The Ballad of Valentine

Alison Jackson ♥ illustrated by Tricia Tusa

PUFFIN BOOKS

PUFFIN BOOKS
Published by the Penguin Group
Penguin Young Readers Group, 345 Hudson Street, New York, New York 10014, U.S.A.
Penguin Group (Canada), 90 Eglinton Avenue East, Suite 700, Toronto, Ontario, Canada M4P 2Y3 (a division of Pearson Penguin Canada Inc.)
Penguin Books Ltd, 80 Strand, London WC2R 0RL, England
Penguin Ireland, 25 St Stephen's Green, Dublin 2, Ireland (a division of Penguin Books Ltd)
Penguin Group (Australia), 250 Camberwell Road, Camberwell, Victoria 3124, Australia (a division of Pearson Australia Group Pty Ltd)
Penguin Books India Pvt Ltd, 11 Community Centre, Panchsheel Park, New Delhi - 110 017, India
Penguin Group (NZ), Cnr Airborne and Rosedale Roads, Albany, Auckland 1310, New Zealand (a division of Pearson New Zealand Ltd)
Penguin Books (South Africa) (Pty) Ltd, 24 Sturdee Avenue, Rosebank, Johannesburg 2196, South Africa

Registered Offices: Penguin Books Ltd, 80 Strand, London WC2R 0RL, England

First published in the United States of America by Dutton Children's Books, a division of Penguin Young Readers Group, 2002
Published by Puffin Books, a division of Penguin Young Readers Group, 2006

1 3 5 7 9 10 8 6 4 2

THE LIBRARY OF CONGRESS HAS CATALOGED THE DUTTON CHILDREN'S BOOKS EDITION AS FOLLOWS:
Jackson, Alison.
The ballad of Valentine / by Alison Jackson; illustrated by Tricia Tusa. p. cm.
Summary: An ardent suitor tries various means of communication, from smoke signals to Morse code to skywriting, in order to get his message to his Valentine.
ISBN: 0-525-46720-3 (hc)

[1. Valentines—Fiction. 2. Stories in rhyme.] I. Tusa, Tricia, ill. II. Title.
PZ8.3.J13435 Bal 2001 [E]—dc21 2001042737

Puffin Books ISBN 0-14-240400-4

Manufactured in China

For Steve, my one and only valentine

—A. J.

For my sister, Nana Banana

—T. T.

N
E
S
W

In a cabin, in a canyon,
Near a mountain laced with pine,
Lived a girl who was my sweetheart,
And her name was Valentine.

Oh my darling, oh my darling,
Oh my darling Valentine,

I have written forty letters,
But you've never read a line.

Gave the letters to a mailman
To deliver, rain or shine.

But he couldn't find your address,

So I penned this valentine.
Then I trained a homing pigeon
And attached my note with twine.

But he flew to Madagascar,
Where he dropped your valentine.

Valentine's
Madagascar

So I built a raging bonfire,
Sent a black and smoky rhyme.

But a cyclone stole the message,
And it vanished one more time.

Next I tapped a note in Morse code,
Asking you to please be mine.
But the signal hit a blizzard
As it crossed the county line.

UNITED STATES MAIL
Post Office
Valentine

Then I rented out a mail car
On the westward railroad line.

FLOUR
sugar

But the train derailed in Denver,
Leaving letters strewn behind.

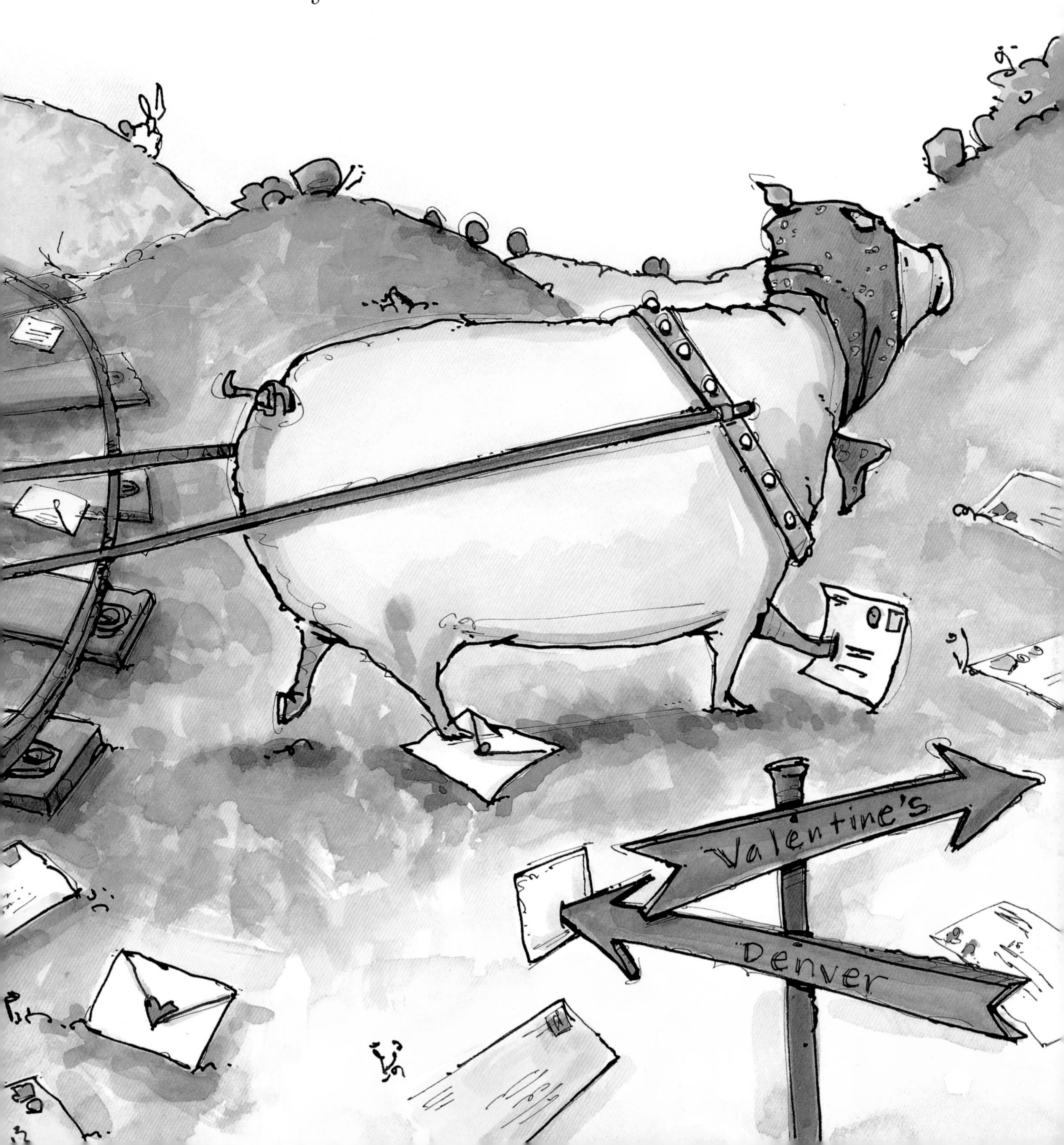

Paid a rider on a pony,
But his filly wouldn't mind.
Bucked him clear to Arizona,
Where he's now been reassigned.

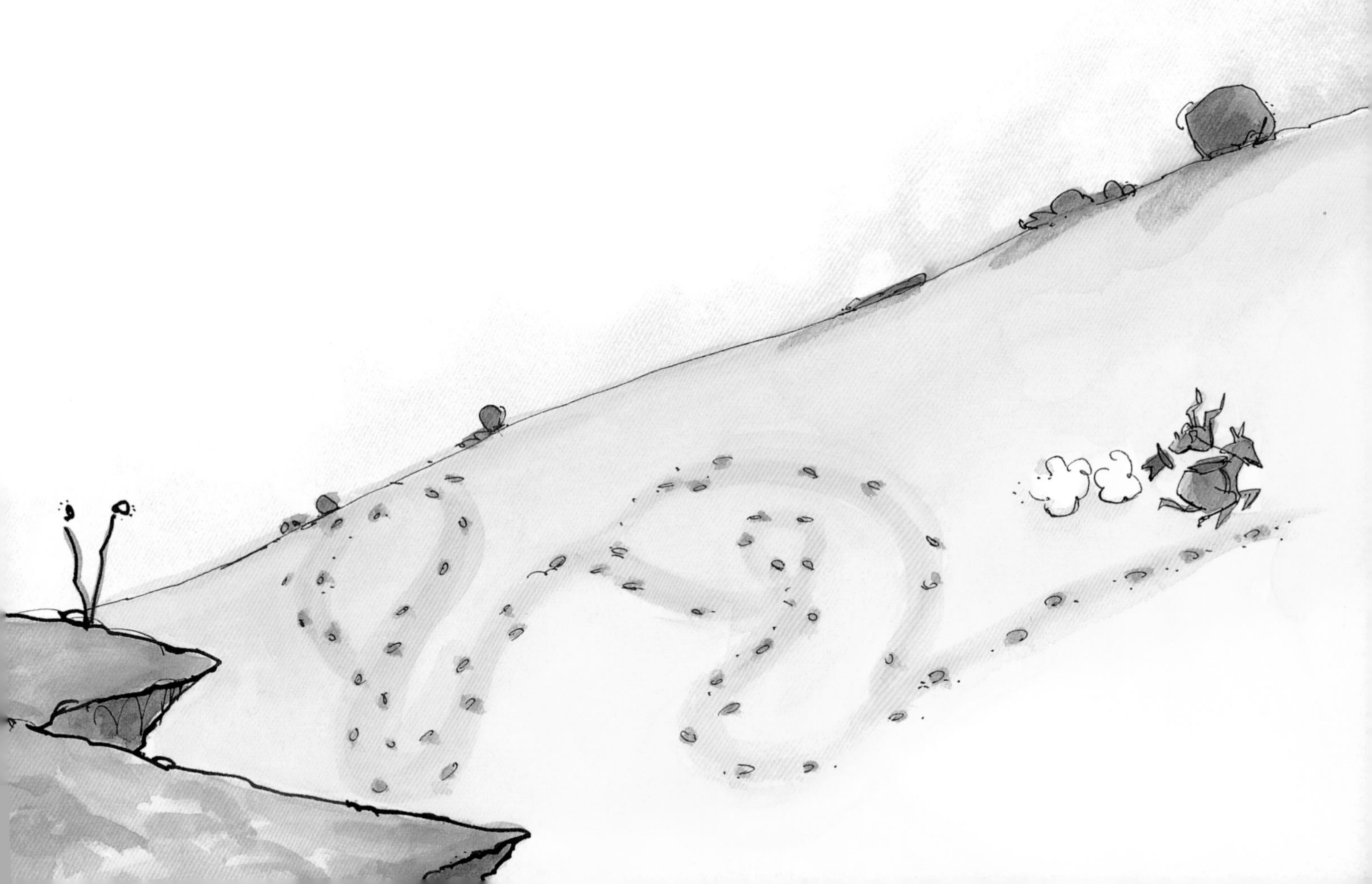

Bought an airplane, wrote a message
With a big heart underlined.
But the wind erased three letters,
And you're now my –al–n–ine.

FLOUR

Tied my message to a boulder
With a sentimental rhyme.
But it rolled down into quicksand.
Now your valentine is slime.

Well, I'm not much of a writer,
But I tried to drop a line.
If you ever get this message,

Will you be my VALENTINE?